Puffin Books

JASON BROWN – FROG

Can you imagine what it's like to be able to swim as well as a
frog? To his delight, Jason Brown gets the chance to find out –
but first he must actually turn into a frog: a giant green slip-
pery frog. Far less embarrassed by his greenness and froggy
features than he had been by his fear of water, Jason hops off
to school to show off his new-found sporting prowess. Wetlegs, the bullying swimming instructor is in for a big surprise.

But winning cups isn't everything, as Jason soon discovers.
After all the excitement of the most extraordinary sports day
ever, he is left with the problem of reversing the spell and
becoming an ordinary boy again . . .

Len Gurd is an artist and cartoonist whose work often appears
in trade newspapers and magazines, especially magazines
about fishing! This is his first book.

LEN GURD

JASON BROWN – FROG

ILLUSTRATED BY TERRY McKENNA

PUFFIN BOOKS

To Luke

PUFFIN BOOKS

Published by the Penguin Group
27 Wrights Lane, London W8 5TZ, England
Viking Penguin Inc., 40 West 23rd Street, New York, New York 10010, USA
Penguin Books Australia Ltd, Ringwood, Victoria, Australia
Penguin Books Canada Ltd, 2801 John Street, Markham, Ontario, Canada L3R 1B4
Penguin Books (NZ) Ltd, 182–190 Wairau Road, Auckland 10, New Zealand

Penguin Books Ltd, Registered Offices: Harmondsworth, Middlesex, England

First published by Viking Kestrel 1989
Published in Puffin Books 1990
10 9 8 7 6 5 4 3 2 1

Text copyright © Len Gurd, 1989
Illustrations copyright © Terry McKenna, 1989
All rights reserved

Made and printed in Great Britain by
Richard Clay Ltd, Bungay, Suffolk

Chapter One

Jason Brown's heart skipped a beat and suddenly he felt a little frightened. The reason for his fear stood before him: Farmer Bell's pond, its cool dark water stretching out before him, sparkling in the early morning sunlight.

Jason should have been on his way to school but instead he found himself standing at this spot more than two miles out of his way.

It was Wednesday, swimming day for the children in his class, which would mean another miserable day with old 'Wetlegs', or to call him by his real name, Mr Bottomley. Mr Bottomley was the swimming instructor, a short-tempered man, who had

made himself the most unpopular person in the whole school because of the way he bullied and poked fun at the children.

The children had nicknamed him 'Wetlegs' because of his habit of sitting on the edge of the swimming-pool with his feet dangling in the water. Jason Brown was his special target.

'Just 'cos I'm scared of the water,' said the boy to himself. 'I can't help it. All he does is tell me off the whole time and make me feel such a fool in front of the others.'

This was the reason Jason had taken a path in the opposite direction from his school; he just couldn't face another Wednesday with Wetlegs.

Jason thought of all the good times he had spent at the pond fishing with his pals for newts and tadpoles. Not that they ever caught any – it was just good fun trying.

There was also the added attraction for

the children of 'Jaws'. Jaws was the name they called the large pike that was supposed to dwell in the pond's depths. Although it had never been seen by any of them they had all heard of it and its supposed victims, which were said to be everything from moorhens to swans, and even, someone had said, Farmer Bell's pet Alsatian, which had mysteriously disappeared. The children loved it all; the thrill of the unknown danger drew them to the spot like a magnet. Swimming, of

course, was out of the question. None of them would dare enter the water even on the hottest of summer days. This suited Jason, who didn't have to worry about his fear of water and embarrassing himself in front of the others.

Jason felt a tingle of excitement. Never had he approached this spot alone before. The water seemed unchanged from his last visit. He walked round to the far bank where the sun cast his shadow across the water. From here he could see small fish dimpling the surface of the pond. He looked carefully into the water's depths, hoping, or rather fearing, to catch a glimpse of the monster pike. He was relieved when, after close inspection, nothing sinister met his gaze.

'I bet it's not true,' he thought hopefully. A slight movement beneath him made him jump. There, in the shallows at his feet,

were dozens of tadpoles clustering around some weed. Jason bent lower to investigate.

He watched as one of the tadpoles detached itself from the others and, with a quick dart, was on the bottom, its head resting against a small stone. The ease with which it carried out this movement amazed Jason. This, and the weight of the satchel he carried containing his towel and swimming trunks, reminded the boy of where he was supposed to be heading that morning. His heart sank at the thought of Wetlegs embarrassing him while he floundered in

the shallow end of the pool. Wetlegs
seemed to enjoy having someone in this
situation.

'You horrible boy,' he would say. 'Get
your horrible little feet off the bottom and
swim. You're not sitting at home on your
backside watching telly now!' Then he
would start to embarrass Jason, saying that
he was nothing but a silly boy who should
be learning with the three-year-olds in their
paddling-pool.

The more he went on, the harder it was for
Jason to do anything. At the sound of the

swimming instructor's voice, Jason would
feel as if his feet were glued to the bottom of
the pool. Try as he might, he couldn't make
himself lift them. This made Wetlegs poke
fun at him even more, which of course
made things worse. Many times Jason
would have to force back tears.

'I can't face another swimming lesson,' he
thought, 'and it will be worse today. I'm
supposed to enter for my twenty-five-metre

certificate and I can't swim a stroke!' He thought of the swimming instructor and how he would make him seem foolish in front of the others. This thought made him very angry.

'That Wetlegs!' he cried out loud, 'I could . . .' He swung his leg in a kicking motion. His foot came into contact with something hard.

'Ouch!' he cried. 'That hurt.' Looking down he saw an old red house brick that had been concealed by the grass. It was then that he saw something else, glittering brightly but partly hidden. Jason reached out towards it. Whoosh! Something green and quite large leapt out of its hiding-place. Jason stepped back, startled. It was a very large, very green frog, and whatever had been glistening was attached to its head. Splash, it was in the water and swimming strongly towards the centre of the pool.

Chapter Two

King Frog was extremely angry. Because of
some ill-behaved boy, he was now having
to swim at the most dangerous time of the
day. King Frog never swam at this time, for
he knew that it was then that the pike fed.
With a darting glance over his shoulder he
kicked his powerful rear legs with all his
strength, trying not only to cross this
dangerous water as quickly as he could, but
also to put as great a distance as possible
between himself and the inconsiderate boy
who had so rudely awakened him.

A long dark shadow slipped from its
hiding place behind a sunken tree trunk.
With glinting eyes it sped towards its prey,
the old enemy, King Frog.

Throughout that morning, the pike had been searching for food without much success. All she had managed was a couple of small roach that had done no more than whet her appetite. Earlier, a moorhen had been searching a lily pad for food himself, when the pike had decided to make him her main course. Fortunately for the moorhen, the pike had, in her haste, misjudged the strike and only managed a mouthful of lily leaves, which had done nothing for her appetite and left her in a foul mood. Now here was her chance to put her mood and her hunger to rights. She was now within striking distance of her old enemy, King Frog.

King Frog's sharp instincts told him, without turning his head, that the pike was almost upon him.

'Jumping tadpoles,' he thought to himself, 'I should have known better than

to let myself get into such a fix.' His bright
mind worked quickly. 'What can I do? Can't
use magic – need my crown on dry land for
that. Can't outswim Pike – she's too fast.'
Suddenly the shock of it came to him. There
was nothing he could do but accept his fate
gracefully like the king he was. His
thoughts were interrupted as he bumped
into something floating on the surface. A
waterlily leaf, one of those detached when
the pike had made her bid for the moorhen,
had been slowly floating across the pond's
surface. King Frog quickly clambered on to it.

'No good for protection,' he thought, 'but at least from up here I can look down at the old brute and curse her before she makes a meal of me.'

The pike could hardly believe her luck. Here was her hated enemy easily within her grasp, and without anything except a waterlily leaf to protect him.

The pike thought of all the times this old King had foiled her efforts to make meals of younger, less wise frogs.

'No more,' she thought. 'One quick snap and I'll be mistress of the pond.'

Jason had been watching the frog's progress, envying the way the creature, with hardly any effort, propelled itself through the water. Suddenly the frog put on speed as if something was chasing it. Jason stared in fascination as the frog reached the loose waterlily leaf and hoisted itself on to it. As Jason watched, a long dark shape appeared and stopped within inches of the leaf.

'Jaws!' gasped Jason, 'So it is true.' The boy's legs turned to jelly as he ran his eyes along the length of the large pike. 'It's longer than I am tall,' he said to himself unbelievingly.

The pike moved forward until its nose was touching the leaf. Jason stood there, unable to move, wondering what would happen.

'Oh no!' It quickly dawned on the boy that the pike intended to eat the frog. The frog seemed unafraid and was staring the big fish in the eye. 'That frog has courage,' thought Jason. 'If that was me I'd be screaming for help.'

As Jason stepped back for a better view, his foot knocked against something. 'The old brick,' gasped the boy. Without thinking, he picked it up and with all his strength he threw it in the direction of the two in the water.

Whoosh. The pike had sensed something coming and had sunk just below the surface. This saved her from receiving the full force of the missile. Even so, it gave her a hefty clout on the top of her head. The big fish lost her senses and sank along with the brick to the bed of the pond.

The force of the brick hitting the water had sent King Frog and the waterlily leaf somersaulting through the air.

'Very undignified,' thought the King as he landed on his back in the water. Splat, the waterlily leaf landed on top of him, blocking out his view completely. The King dived to get clear of the leaf and saw the pike lying dazed on the bottom of the pond.

'Saved,' said the King to himself. 'It must have been that boy.' He swam back to the surface and saw the boy standing there looking rather frightened.

'Blow!' said the King, out loud.

Chapter Three

King Frog made his way back towards the spot where the boy stood. He had a duty to perform and was angered at the thought of it.

'Toothless toads,' he cursed, 'if it hadn't been for that stupid boy I would still be in the shelter of an old house brick dreaming of better times.' Pulling himself up on to the bank he came to rest at last, panting, at the boy's feet. Jason looked down. Never had he seen such a large frog. There, gleaming on its head, was the object which had first caught his attention – a tiny crown!

With bulging, unbelieving eyes, the boy reached down to pick up the frog.

'Keep your hands off me,' hissed King Frog. Jason jumped back in fright.

'You can speak,' the boy stammered.

'Of course I can speak,' said the King sharply, annoyed that anyone would have the cheek even to think that he could not. 'And in six of the different languages of men,' he added proudly.

'Golly!' exclaimed Jason. The boy was no longer frightened. 'What on earth can a frog do to harm me,' he thought to himself. The King was eyeing him carefully now. Jason stared back.

'What's that on your head, frog?' Jason asked, looking curiously at the glittering jewel.

'My crown,' said the King crossly. 'What a stupid question. What did you think it was? Don't you know a king when you see one?'

'Sorry, your majesty,' said Jason cheekily, at the same time giving an exaggerated bow. The boy felt no fear at all now.

King Frog fumed. 'You cheeky young whipper-snapper. Who do you think you are?' he snarled. His eyes bulged as he took a deep breath and blew himself up to three times his normal size. Jason suddenly felt frightened again and was lost for words.

'How old are you?' said the King.

'T-t-ten and a half,' stuttered the boy.

'Well,' said the King, 'I am three hundred and thirty-seven years, four months, three days and . . .' he looked up at the position of the sun and added, 'eight and a half hours old, which makes me your senior as well as your better.'

Jason hung his head while the King, who had now returned to his normal size, went on.

'There I was, having a peaceful sleep beneath my brick, when along you come and kick it. What are you doing here anyway? It is a school day and I expect you children down here only on holidays, weekends and after school, at which time I am sure to be out of the way. You are playing truant, I'll be bound.'

'School hasn't started yet,' said Jason, knowing it to be untrue.

'Well, it's going to start without you by the look of things,' said the King sharply. Before Jason could think of a reply, the King asked, 'Well, what is it you want?'

'I don't know what you mean,' replied Jason, puzzled.

'Oh, give me strength,' sighed the King, burying his head in his flippers. 'Don't you know anything?'

Jason, looking bewildered, said, 'I still don't know what you mean, sir.'

'Don't call me sir,' said the King, looking angry again. 'Your majesty, or King

Frog will do nicely.' He looked
Jason up and down and then added,
'Any fool knows that they are
automatically granted a wish when they
save the life of a member of the royal frog
line, even in your case, when you were the
one who caused my life to be in danger.'

'I'm sorry, your majesty,' whispered
Jason.

'So you should be,' replied the frog.
'Well, come on, what is it you want? I
haven't got all day!'

Jason stood for a while, lost for words.
Eventually he said, 'I don't know.'

For the second time, King Frog buried
his head in his flippers and sighed with
exasperation. At last he looked up and
said quietly to the boy, 'Surely there is
something you want, more than anything
else in the world. Just say the word and,
if it is possible, it is yours!'

A look of understanding crossed Jason's face. 'Yes, yes,' he blurted out. 'I would like to swim like you.'

'Is that all,' said the King, a surprised look on his face. 'I thought the least you would ask for would be a lifetime's supply of sweets.'

'No, no,' said Jason, 'to swim as well as you would be super.'

The King studied him carefully for a long

while, without saying a word. Then he said quite deliberately, 'The human body is not capable of swimming like a frog's; it may have two arms and two legs which are similar, but their shape is all wrong. The toes are too short and not webbed, and neither are the fingers. The head and body shape are also completely out of proportion.'

'So you can't do it,' said Jason, disappointed.

'I didn't say that,' said the King, 'but it will mean me turning you into a frog. You would remain the same inside, naturally, but on the outside you would be a frog and, because of your large size, you would be able to swim faster than any frog in the world. Is that what you want?'

A wide smile spread across Jason's face and his eyes gleamed. 'Yes,' he said quickly, 'please do it.'

'It is not as straightforward as that,' said the King. 'What about your family, your parents? What would they say?'

'They wouldn't mind,' said the boy, without thinking.

'They would,' said the King thoughtfully. 'They might even reject you and put you out of your home. You would probably starve. I wouldn't want that on my conscience.'

Jason's heart sank for a moment. He had imagined himself winning the twenty-five-metre swimming certificate at least.

King Frog was speaking again, and there was a mischievous gleam in his eyes. 'I could of course arrange for your whole family to change with you; that way they would accept you. Your parents might not like it though.'

'They wouldn't mind,' said Jason, again not bothering to think about how they might feel.

'Are you sure?' said the King with a knowing smile on his face.

'Positive,' Jason insisted.

'OK,' said the King, 'consider it done.'

With that he took the tiny gold crown from his head and, turning it upside down, placed it on the ground. Then he started to hop round the crown, chanting something quietly to himself. Suddenly he stopped and, turning to Jason, he said, 'Apart from your parents, is there anyone else in your family?'

'Yes,' replied Jason, 'my baby brother, Lucas.'

'How old is he?' asked the King.

'Four months,' replied Jason, quickly totting it up on his fingers.

'Not old enough to be a frog yet,' said the King. 'Never mind, I know what to do with him.' He continued to hop around chanting. After some time he stopped.

'That's done,' he sighed. 'It's a long time since I've granted a wish.' The King replaced the tiny crown on his head. 'I'd better be off,' he said, and with that, he took a long hop in the direction of some stinging-nettles. 'By the way,' he called over his shoulder, 'if you want to reverse the spell, you do the usual thing. Don't forget.' Another long hop and he disappeared into the nettles.

Jason stood there alone. 'I wonder what he meant by the usual thing,' he thought, feeling somewhat confused.

Chapter Four

For a long time Jason stood thinking. A large dragonfly buzzing close to his head snapped him back to reality. 'Must have been dreaming,' he thought.

He felt a strange sensation in his body. It did not feel the same any more. He stared across the pond. A kingfisher, which before had been hidden from him, now stood out bright and clear in its hiding-place. He could even pick out the individual insects crawling on the leaves near the bird.

He reached up to rub his eyes, and the objects in front of him made him start. Instead of the familiar small hands there were two large green flippers.

'It was true, then,' said Jason, speaking his thoughts aloud. With his heart beating madly he rushed to the edge of the pond to look at his reflection. The tadpoles that had been disturbed earlier were again happily feeding on the piece of weed. At the sudden appearance of Jason they scattered, leaving the surface of the water rippling. As Jason watched the water began to clear and, slowly, a green head formed, which appeared to be sticking out of his red T-shirt.

There in the water was the unmistakable reflection of a large frog. Jason did a little jump for joy and found himself five metres in the air. He landed in an untidy heap and giggled. He jumped again, and again, all around the pond, laughing to himself all

the time. 'I'm a frog,' he yelled, 'A frog, a frog.' Jason looked at the water; it looked very inviting and he felt no fear of it whatsoever. He was just about to leap in when he remembered where he should be at that moment.

Normally, there was no way he could ever have got back to school in time for the swimming lesson, but now, with his newly gained strength, he found himself racing across country to the distant school building, taking the hedges and streams in giant leaps. Even so, he was late for the register and he arrived just as the children were lining up in the playground to be led to the local swimming-pool by the dreaded swimming instructor. 'OK, you nasty lot, let's get moving,' shouted Wetlegs. The line of children moved forward, many of them casting an uneasy glance in the direction of their instructor.

Mr Sykes, the PE teacher, had gone on ahead to ensure that everything was in order at the pool ready for the children's arrival; or so he said, but really it was because he couldn't face walking the short distance to the pool with Mr Bottomley, listening to him bullying and poking fun at the children. No one noticed Jason as he joined the end of the column.

'Stop talking,' yelled Wetlegs. 'Keep in line there. Keep your eyes to the front, Kefford.' The orders and abuse poured out in a never-ending stream as the children moved in a long column along School Lane to the pool.

The building was soon in sight, and as the children entered, Jason hung back until he saw his chance to slip in unnoticed. They always had to use the same changing cubicles – this was one of Wetlegs's orders – so Jason now slipped quietly into his. It was next to the cubicle of his best friend, Willie Rodgers.

Jason and Willie had known each other since they were babies; they were neighbours and inseparable friends.

'Willie,' whispered Jason through a crack in the wooden cubicle wall, 'it's me, Jason.'

'Hello, Jase,' Willie whispered in reply. 'Thought you were skipping school today.'

'I was,' Jason whispered back cautiously. 'I went down to Farmer Bell's pond.'

'What, on your own? gasped Willie.

'Yes,' replied Jason. 'Something funny happened to me down there.' Willie listened in stunned silence as Jason related the whole strange story. When he had finished Willie started to giggle. 'You don't 'arf tell 'em,' he said at last.

'But it's true. Look through the crack,' said Jason. Willie looked through the crack and his giggles turned into uncontrollable

laughter. From what seemed a long way off, Wetlegs screamed.

'Quiet, you horrors.'

For a while, the boys remained silent, then Jason whispered, 'What shall I say about my appearance, Willie?'

Willie thought for a while and then said, 'Say you've been ill, the mumps, frogitis, anything.'

Before they could discuss it further, Wetlegs was blowing his whistle, which was the signal for them all to assemble at the pool side. Jason and Willie hung back behind the others. One or two of the boys noticed Jason and started to mutter and giggle amongst themselves. A great bellow from Wetlegs soon brought them to order.

When all was quiet, Wetlegs began. 'Right, you horrible lot. Today's the day when those children who haven't already got one go in for their twenty-five-metre certificates. For those of you who have already done it, it will be the fifty-metre. There will be no excuses – you will all pass!' He hesitated, looking around at the assembled faces, 'That is to say, all but one,' he added. 'Where is that horrible boy?' No one answered. 'Brown,' yelled Wetlegs, 'step forward!' Jason pushed his way through the children to the front. His heart was pounding at the thought of coming face to face with the awful swimming instructor again.

'Yes, sir,' said Jason feebly. Wetlegs looked at him long and hard. 'What's the matter with your head, Brown?' he said questioningly.

'Been ill, sir,' Jason muttered.

'Hmm.' Wetlegs stared at him with suspicious eyes. The boys next to Jason started to giggle. Wetlegs, turning purple with rage, rounded on the giggling children and screamed them into silence. At last, having expended his rage on the offenders, he turned once more to Jason.

'Why aren't you in the water, boy? Get in

at once!' he bellowed. So keen was he to get the boy into the water, he forgot to question him further about his unusual appearance.

Jason turned to the pool. The water looked clean and pleasant. No longer did it hold any fear for him. Looking to his left he saw the high diving-board.

'Right,' he thought, 'here goes.' Before anyone could say anything Jason was along the pool-side and half-way up the diving-board steps. Wetlegs blew his whistle and screamed, 'Come back here, you stupid

boy! It's the shallow end you want!'

Jason ignored him and continued to climb. On reaching the top he walked out on to the edge of the board and looked down. The water looked so inviting. Everyone watched him silently. Even Wetlegs was at a loss for words. Mr Sykes, looking worried, had started to climb the diving-board steps after him.

The children gasped as Jason, balancing

lightly on the edge, suddenly leapt into the
air, did a triple somersault and straightened
his body just in time to cut into the water
almost without disturbing it. Everyone
was looking at the spot where he had
disappeared when a shout from Willie
made them all turn around. Jason had
appeared at the shallow end of the pool!

Without waiting he did a backward flip,
twisted and began to swim, his legs and
arms moving so fast they were just a blur.
The water behind his rear flippers was
churned into a white foam.

Wetlegs stood on the edge of the pool
with his face becoming redder and redder.
He just could not believe his eyes. The

children were crazy with excitement; running up and down the side of the pool, they tried to keep up with Jason as he swam one length after another. Soon they had to give up and could do no more than cheer and shout encouragement. Mr Sykes was looking unbelievingly at his stop-watch – he had been timing Jason. 'Amazing,' he said out loud. 'The lad's been doing over sixty miles an hour, which is impossible.'

There was no doubt about it. Jason clocked up five miles in no time at all. It was on this announcement that Wetlegs, his rage getting the better of him, slipped and fell into the pool.

Spluttering to the surface, the big man yelled, 'Help! Can't swim!' Jason swam towards him and, grabbing him by the collar, found the non-swimming instructor had fainted, which made it easy for him to tow the great weight to the side, and that was how, in addition to winning every distance certificate, he also won the life-saving certificate.

Mr Sykes, with the help of some of the bigger boys, pulled Wetlegs up on to the side. 'He needs the kiss of life,' exclaimed the PE teacher. There were no volunteers. 'Looks as if I'll have to do it myself then,' said the teacher reluctantly. Soon he had Wetlegs gasping and spluttering for breath. The big man sat up, looking very pale, still at a loss for words. Mr Sykes said, 'We will have to get you to the doctor, Bottomley.'

The big man did not answer. He just sat there in a daze. Two of the pool attendants came forward and offered to escort Mr Bottomley to a doctor. When they had gone, Mr Sykes called everyone together. 'I'm afraid we will have to call the swimming lesson off today,' he said. The children looked disappointed for, with

Wetlegs gone, they had been looking forward to a nice peaceful swim. 'You can all go early,' said the teacher. The children cheered, and clapped Jason on the back. He felt so good he didn't know what to say. All he could do was grin at them, a big froggy grin from ear to ear. At last, when most of the boys had gone to their cubicles to change, Mr Sykes took Jason over to the corner where all the certificates lay on a table. The teacher carefully made them all out to Jason. 'Well done,' said the teacher. 'Now run along home with the others while I go and see how Mr Bottomley is getting on at the doctor's.' Studying Jason carefully for a moment, he added. 'And I don't think it would be a bad idea if you went to the doctor yourself – you look very peculiar.'

Jason began walking home, the certificates firmly in his flippers. So intent was he on getting home that he did not

notice Willie trying to keep up with his long froggy strides.

'Can't wait to show mum and dad,' he thought to himself. The certificates in his hand looked so important, each individual one tied with a scarlet ribbon.

Chapter Five

Mrs Brown was having a very busy morning. Baby Lucas was unusually quiet, she thought, as she hung his nappies on the washing-line.

A piercing scream came from the baby's room. Dropping the nappies, Mrs Brown flew into the house. It was at this precise moment that King Frog's magic took effect, but so intent was she on reaching her screaming infant that she did not realize she had taken the stairs in a single hop. She reached the child's cot, from where the wailing sobs were now coming; the baby was obviously in great distress. The sight that met her eyes made her freeze to the spot. There in the cot, where her baby had been, was a large tadpole, and it was crying with the unmistakable sound of her baby Lucas. 'Oh, you poor thing,' cried Mrs Brown, suddenly coming to her senses. She swept the baby up into her arms, and the sobs started to die as she rocked him to and fro.

'Must have been that baby food I gave him last night,' she said to herself. She found his dummy in his cot and put it in his mouth, and the sobs died altogether. She laid the baby back into his cot and rushed to the telephone.

'Must phone Bill,' she said, in a distressed tone. But the hand that gripped the receiver was not the hand she knew. A large green flipper had taken its place! Mrs Brown dropped the receiver, stifled a scream and rushed to the bathroom. There in the mirror, where her own face should have been, was the face of a large frog. The

poor woman fainted and fell backwards
into the bath.

Bill Brown, Jason's father, was a
fishmonger. He enjoyed his job managing
the wet-fish shop, which belonged to
Councillor Renshaw, the town's mayor.
'It's not a bad job,' he would think to
himself, 'despite that old miser Renshaw
and his miserable wife.' He was at the back
of the shop cleaning some cod that had
been delivered earlier in the day. He was
working alone that week, as his assistant
was away on his summer holiday. The shop

bell rang and someone entered. 'That will be Councillor Renshaw's wife,' he thought. 'Always comes in Wednesday morning for a piece of fresh salmon.' Wiping his hands, he walked out into the shop.

It was at this moment that King Frog's magic took effect on him. The fat mayoress was leaning into the shop window, her short, stubby fingers prodding everything. Hearing Bill enter the shop behind her she snapped, 'Is this fresh?', her fingers jabbing at a tray of salmon.

'Yes, of course, Mrs Renshaw,' replied Mr Brown. The fat woman turned to face him, and was just about to add that it had better be, when her words dried in her mouth.

'Keep away from me, you ugly brute!' she screamed, suddenly finding her voice.

For a moment Jason's father did not know what to say, and then his temper snapped. 'Don't you call me an ugly brute,'

he shouted, taking a step nearer to the now
petrified woman. This was too much for
Mrs Renshaw, and with a blood-curdling
scream she dropped her handbag and
rushed out of the shop – into the arms of
her husband, who had been parking the
car.

Councillor Renshaw charged into the shop. 'What have you been doing to my wife?' he shouted, but as soon as he saw the large frog in its white overall he was struck dumb.

Mr Brown was still fuming at what he thought was an unwarranted attack by Mrs Renshaw. 'I may work for you, but that does not give your wife the right to insult me,' he said. The familiar-sounding voice made the mayor look more closely.

'It is you then, Brown. What is the idea of wearing that silly mask and frightening people? It won't do our trade any good, you know!' exclaimed the mayor.

'Don't you insult me as well, you silly old codger!' snarled Mr Brown angrily.

'Silly old codger am I! I'll show you. You're sacked! Sacked, do you hear me!' The mayor was fuming.

'That suits me,' said Mr Brown, 'but

before I go, here is your wife's salmon.'
Picking up the tray of salmon, the
ex-fishmonger tipped it over the mayor's
head and stormed out of the shop.

When Mrs Brown came round, her baby
was still screaming; she pulled herself out
of the bath and went to him. A quick glance
in the mirror as she passed confirmed that
she had not been dreaming.

The baby was in a terrible state by this
time, screaming loudly. His mother picked
him up and found that he felt very dry and
warm. 'Do you want your nappy changed?'
she cooed to the unfamiliar shape she held
in her arms. Taking the child down into the
lounge she laid him on the floor and
removed his outer garments.

'Mummy will change your nappy,' she
whispered softly to the howling baby. It
was then that she realized that her child did

not have legs any more – just a long dark
tail where they had been. Try as she might
she could not make his nappy stay on.

'It was bad enough keeping a nappy on
when you had two legs,' she said. 'I'm sure
I don't know how to keep one on you now.'

The baby was still screaming and, on
hearing her voice, he screamed even
louder.

It was at this point that Jason walked in.
'Hello, mum,' he said, holding up his

certificates proudly for her to see.

Mrs Brown did not see anything except the head of her elder son. 'Not you as well,' she sobbed. This was too much for her. She sat down heavily in a chair.

Lucas, lying on the floor, continued to scream. Jason looked closely at him. 'Cor, mum, do you think he will grow legs?' he said. Mrs Brown could not take any more. Burying her head in her flippers, she joined the baby in great wailing sobs that could be heard at the end of the street. Jason stood there, not knowing what to say, his certificates momentarily forgotten. This was how Mr Brown came home and found them.

Chapter Six

It took Mr Brown two hours to quieten his wife and stop her crying, but the baby could not be stopped. He cried and cried until his parents thought he must be seriously ill. Dr Shah was telephoned and he said that he would be there as soon as he possibly could.

Jason spent this period keeping out of the way and going over in his mind the events of the morning. He had not realized his parents would take it so badly. He did not mind being a frog; up until now it had been great fun. He was sure Lucas would find it fun too, when he stopped crying. It upset him seeing his mother in such distress, and on top of this, his father had lost his job.

Jason did not realize how serious this was. Soon his mind wandered on to other things. His certificates – where was he going to hang them? He decided that the wall opposite his bed would be best. In that position, he could lie in bed and look at them. He had just fixed the last one to the wall when a call from his mother summoned him downstairs. Dr Shah's car had pulled up outside and his father wanted the doctor to examine the whole family.

Dr Shah looked at them all closely. 'Well,' he said at last, 'I have never seen anything like this in all my medical career.' Baby Lucas wailed louder and louder.

'Please examine the baby first,' said Mrs Brown desperately.

The doctor took out his stethoscope and held it against the baby. Carefully, the doctor covered most of the child's body,

listening carefully and shaking his head slowly. Every few seconds he would mutter something to himself. Finally, he took his stethoscope from his ears and, looking at the parents, said, 'I'm sorry, but I think we will have to put this child in hospital for extensive tests.' A large sob escaped the lips of Mrs Brown. Mr Brown comforted her.

'Do you think it's for the best, doctor?' he said quietly.

Before the doctor could answer, Jason butted in. 'I know what's wrong with him, dad,' he said.

The three adults turned and looked at Jason. At last his father said, 'Well, what is it, son?'

Without answering, Jason went to the kitchen cupboard. At the bottom was a very large jar which his mother had been keeping for pickling. Jason carried it to the kitchen sink and filled it with water. Placing it on the kitchen table, he said, 'That's what Lucas wants, mum.'

'He can't drink all that,' said his mother.

'No, no,' said Dr Shah, suddenly realizing what the baby's problem was, 'I know what the young man means.' He picked up the baby and gently lowered him into the jar of water. Lucas wiggled his little tail and swam around the jar cooing, big bubbles of joy coming from his mouth.

After a while it seemed that Lucas was no longer in distress.

'Is he going to be all right?' asked Mrs Brown anxiously.

'I think so,' said the doctor, holding the stethoscope against the jar. 'Yes,' he said after a while, 'the baby seems fine now, he just needed water. Now, starting with Jason, I think I had better examine the rest of you.'

The doctor examined them all thoroughly, muttering to himself all the time. At last he had finished and Mr Brown asked him what the verdict was. The doctor shook his head, not knowing what to say.

'I know what it is,' said Mrs Brown, 'it's that fish we all ate yesterday! I thought it tasted funny.'

The doctor looked at her steadily for a moment and said, 'Did the baby eat any of it?'

'Why, no, of course not, he's not old enough, doctor,' said Mrs Brown in surprise.

'Then it's not the fish that did it, and to be honest, Mr and Mrs Brown, I don't know what has caused this. If I didn't know better I would say you all had turned into frogs.' Jason slipped out of the room, ashamed at last of the disaster he had brought upon his parents.

Jason was awake bright and early next morning. The noise of the birds singing and the early-morning sunshine streaming through the window made him feel good. His gaze wandered around the bedroom walls. There, opposite him, lined up on the wall, were all his swimming certificates.

'So I wasn't dreaming,' he said to himself. He jumped out of bed and ran into the bathroom. A quick look in the mirror convinced him that it had not been a dream. He dashed downstairs to find his parents sitting around the kitchen table watching the large jar in which baby Lucas, still

looking very happy, was swimming round and round.

'Didn't you go to bed?' he asked his tired-looking parents.

'No, son,' said his father, looking at him with his very large, sad, frog's eyes. 'Your mum and I sat up all night. We were afraid your little brother might drown.'

'He won't drown, dad,' said the boy smiling knowingly.

His father looked at him very hard and said, 'I think you know more about this than meets the eye.'

'No I don't, dad, honest,' said Jason, feeling guilty telling lies to his parents, but what could he do? They would never believe him anyway.

'No school today, Jason,' said his mother.

'Oh . . . mum, why?' Jason was upset at not being able to show off his new powers.

'The doctor said you were to stay in until

he sorts out our problem,' said his mother.

Jason was very bored for the rest of the day. The garden was not long enough to practise his jumping, the bath was not big enough to swim in. Nothing seemed to interest him except playing with his little brother, and this had only been possible when his parents were not in the room. Jason, using a long stick, had stirred the water in the jar as fast as he could, sending the youngster flying round and round. Every time his little brother passed he would pull faces at him; the baby loved it.

Jason was about to take their games a step further and put Lucas in the washing-machine when his mother walked in.

'Don't you think we have enough trouble without you making things worse,' she said. Jason hung his head and waited for his punishment. 'Get up to your room and stay there,' said his mother sharply.

'Always the same,' thought the boy as he climbed the stairs. 'Just start to have some fun and I'm sent to bed.'

The following day followed a similar pattern. When Jason's mother caught him trying to feed his baby brother by dropping worms into the jar, she became quite hysterical. 'It's school for you again on Monday, I don't care what the doctor says.'

From her tone, Jason knew that his mother meant what she said and he was very pleased, though he went to great lengths not to show it.

Chapter Seven

Monday morning seemed to take a long time coming. To Jason, Saturday and Sunday were just a big bore, as were Thursday and Friday. He had managed to have a quiet word with Willie, urging him to keep their secret about King Frog.

From his vantage point, a bush half-way along the school lane, Jason watched and waited. 'They won't be long now,' he said to himself. Jason had surprised his parents by wanting to leave early that morning. 'Can't think what's got into the child,' said his father as he looked through the morning papers to see if there were any job vacancies for frogs. Jason had a very good reason for wanting to leave early that morning, and that reason was now in sight. Approaching along the lane were two girls, Angela Dimmock and Cheryl Kelly. They were in Jason's class and he found it great sport to tease them. He crouched low behind the bush, listening carefully for the sound of their voices. Jason had waited a long time for these two. Most of the other children had passed unaware of his presence. The voices grew louder until at last Jason judged them to be directly opposite him.

'Croak, croak, croak,' came the sound from his lips. He giggled to himself, thinking of the girls' reaction. 'Did you hear that?' said Cheryl in a whisper. 'Yes,' said Angela, 'it sounded like a frog. Perhaps the poor little thing is lost.'

The two girls quietly approached the bush. This was the moment Jason had been waiting for. With an almighty croak, he leapt from his hiding-place, landing on all

fours in front of the two frightened girls.
Taking a deep breath, he blew himself up as
he had seen King Frog do. He knew how
horrible he would look because he had been
practising it all weekend in front of a mirror
at home. The two girls screamed and,
dropping their satchels, fled down the lane
towards the school. Jason, hopping on all
fours and croaking, followed them, keeping
just one pace behind, until at the school gates

he fell in a heap of uncontrollable laughter.

'So you've come back, boy.' It was the voice of the PE teacher, Mr Sykes. Looking down at him, the teacher went on, 'Hope you're feeling better after your illness. I want everyone fit today as it's Sports Day.

Jason had forgotten all about this. 'Can I enter for everything, please, sir?' Jason said with confidence.

'Why of course you can,' said the teacher, looking amazed. It was normally difficult to persuade Jason to enter for any of the events. 'Now run along to your class before you're late,' he added.

Jason entered the classroom. Everyone was already seated behind their desks – that is, everyone except Angela and Cheryl. They were being comforted by Mrs Williams, the form teacher. At the sight of Jason entering, the two girls clung tightly to their teacher.

'It's all right, girls,' said Mrs Williams. 'It's only Jason Brown. I've had a note from his father. It seems poor Jason has probably eaten something that didn't agree with him.'

'He doesn't agree with us much,' came a voice from the back of the classroom. It was big John Kefford, the school bully. The boys around him started to snigger.

'Quiet,' said Mrs Williams sternly. 'I won't have this in my classroom. Jason cannot help his appearance and I will not have anyone here poking fun at him because of it.' She turned to the two girls. 'Now you two can sit down. You can see there is nothing to be frightened of.'

The two girls sat down silently, keeping a watchful eye on Jason at the same time. Jason took his own place, next to Willie. Mrs Williams called the register and reminded the children that after assembly they were to report to the gym, as it was Sports Day.

After assembly, Jason and Willie hurried towards the gym together. 'Have you heard about old Wetlegs?' said Willie. 'He's resigned.'

Jason smiled. 'Good. Good riddance to the old goat,' he replied happily. Willie did not say any more and seemed very embarrassed to be walking with Jason. Jason wondered what was wrong; he and Willie were usually very close friends.

Jason soon forgot Willie's strangeness. Sports Day was under way and, with his new-found confidence, he was determined to compete in everything.

The playing-field was busy that day. Most of the parents were there to see their children competing. Jason's parents had of course stayed at home, too ashamed of their appearance to venture far out of doors.

Looking around for Willie, Jason spotted him lining up with the other competitors to take part in the long jump. As the children each took their turn to jump, Mr Sykes and Mrs Williams would measure the footprints in the sand where they had landed.

Willie was good at jumping and prided himself on being the best in his class. Today was no exception. After his first jump he was leading the rest of the children by nearly a metre, until Jason took his turn. Without any effort Jason ran up and took off. Everyone gasped in astonishment as

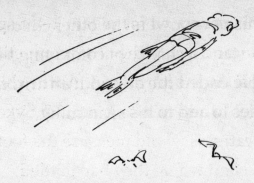

Jason cleared the sandpit and landed gracefully a hundred metres away on the other side of the playing-field.

Mr Sykes said, 'I cannot see any point in carrying on with this event. No one in the world could jump that far.'

Willie looked very upset and walked away. He had been sure he would win the event with his last jump.

Next came the high jump, with Jason jumping so high he became a small speck in the sky. Everyone stood back in amazement as he descended, performing several somersaults on the way.

Needless to say, Jason won every event;

with his new powers the other children didn't stand a chance of competing against him. He ended the day with an armful of trophies to add to his swimming certificates.

The other children seemed to resent Jason and his success. From being the hero of the swimming-pool and everyone's favourite for getting rid of Wetlegs, he was now looked on as a bore and a big-head. The other boys began to taunt him about his looks. Even Angela and Cheryl were no longer afraid of him and laughed at him

with the other girls. Willie had become friendly with big John Kefford and his gang. On approaching them John had told him to 'hop it'. All the boys had thought this hilarious and the school's pet saying became 'Hop it, Brown,' which Jason did not care for.

That first week back at school was a nightmare for Jason. Everyone had deserted him at playtimes and during the evenings after school he was completely alone.

By the end of the week, his parents were in financial trouble. Without any money coming in, they had to go to the Social Security Office. The people there were very rude, and said that frogs were not allowed to draw benefit, and they should try the RSPCA. Jason's pocket-money and sweet allowance was stopped, along with his favourite comics. All the available money was needed for food.

The Saturday and Sunday following that first week went very slowly, giving Jason plenty of time to think about his family's problems. 'If only we could get back to normal,' he thought. His dad could get a job; old Mr Jones in the next village wanted a good fishmonger to run his shop and the job was there for the asking, but not while dad looked as he did – no one would want to buy fish from a frog. His mother could stop worrying about how to fit a nappy on a tadpole and Jason would have his friends back, and have someone to play with again.

No matter how Jason pondered, he could not think of any solution to their problems, except to find King Frog and ask his help. This he resolved to do on the Monday, instead of going to school. He would visit Farmer Bell's pond and ask King Frog to reverse the spell.

Chapter Eight

On Monday Jason left his home for school
as usual, but half-way down the lane,
seeing no one was around, he hopped
smartly over the fence into the adjoining
field, and disappeared in the direction of
Farmer Bell's pond.

As Jason approached, the pond looked
even quieter than normal. The surface was
still and calm, reflecting everything like a
huge mirror. No life was to be seen
anywhere. Jason walked round and round,
looking into the pond's depths and in the
surrounding undergrowth. All the time he
called, 'King Frog, King Frog! Where are
you? Please show yourself.'

There was no sign of King Frog or the

tadpoles which had been in the margin on his last visit. Jason sat down and stifled a sob. After sitting for some time he spoke out loud.

'If you can hear me, King Frog, please help. My family are in trouble and I've lost all my friends.' Jason hung his head to his chest. 'Oh, I wish I knew how to reverse the spell,' he sobbed.

Suddenly the wind picked up. Not in the usual way, but with such force that it nearly blew Jason flat on to his back. It was very unusual – one moment it had been very calm, without even a breeze, and the next the wind was blowing at gale force. Great waves with white foaming crests leapt across the pond towards him. With great difficulty, because his eyes were stinging, Jason looked in the direction from which the wind was coming. In the distance, carried by the wind, was something he

could not take his eyes from. Closer and
closer came the object. It was going to hit
him, there was nothing he could do to stop
it. It was as if he were unable to move. Then
smack, it hit him full in the face, wrapping
itself round his head. In the same instant
the wind stopped and it became dead calm
again. Jason pulled the object from his face;
it was the front page of a local newspaper.

The headlines read, 'Princess to open new school at Milshum.'

'That's it,' cried Jason. 'Why didn't I think of it before? I have to get a real princess to kiss me.' Reading on, he found that the school was to be opened that very morning. He thought of the old fairy-tale his mother had read to him when he was younger, and how the princess had kissed the enchanted frog and it had turned into a prince.

'So that's what the frog meant when he said that to reverse the spell you do "the usual thing".'

The thought of being kissed by a member of the opposite sex did not appeal to Jason too much – it embarrassed him when his mother insisted on kissing him goodbye in front of Willie – but he knew there was no alternative. Jason turned from the pond, and hurried off in the direction of the town of Milshum.

King Frog, from his hiding-place in a bed of stinging-nettles, watched him go. 'That's the second wish I've granted that stupid boy,' he said to himself.

The old frog turned. It was time he went away; he had only stayed on this long because he knew the boy would be back. It would not be safe near the pond any more once the word got around. You could not trust humans to keep things to themselves. With a long hop he disappeared into the hedge on the other side of the stinging-nettles.

Jason soon realized that even with the great speed he was now capable of, it was unlikely that he would reach Milshum in time, but it would give him more speed if he were rid of his clothes. Without hesitation Jason stripped them off and hid them in a bush.

Then he was off again, leaping high hedges, streams, rivers and railway embankments as if they did not exist. At last Jason skidded breathlessly to a halt at the edge of town.

Crowds of people were making their way towards the town centre. All the roads were jammed with traffic going in the same direction. 'I'm not too late then,' thought

Jason to himself. He joined the crowd and, walking at a more leisurely pace, soon regained his breath.

People were looking at him, and talking excitedly. Some were laughing. Others were looking alarmed. Jason realized that without his clothes on he looked more like a giant frog than ever. A large policeman started approaching Jim through the crowd. 'Time I was off,' said Jason aloud. He took a gigantic leap which took him over the roof of a nearby bungalow. He heard the crowd gasp with amazement as he dropped lightly into the garden behind. A small terrier barked angrily and rushed at him, snapping. Jason leapt again and again over the back-garden fences. From windows as he passed he caught glimpses of frightened faces, and heard cries of alarm. From the road came the sound of a police siren.

'Oh dear,' thought the boy. 'What shall I do? I'll be arrested before I can even see the Princess.'

With another long leap he found himself on a small path that led between the rows of houses and gardens. Jason turned and hurried along it away from the road. The path led eventually to a large open area. Jason peered around cautiously, and saw neatly cut grass stretching away into the distance with goal-posts dotted here and there. It was a large sports field. There, in the distance, on the other side of the field, was the unmistakable shape of a new school building.

'That must be it,' said Jason excitedly to himself. He could hear crowds of people cheering at the other side of the building. 'That must be the Princess arriving,' he thought. Hurrying quickly around the school building, Jason soon found himself

at the rear of the large, excited crowd. Policemen were everywhere but there was no sign of the Princess.

'The Princess must be inside opening the school,' he thought. 'I must catch her on the way back.'

He saw a large black car by the side of the road. There were crowds all around it. Leading from the car to the school's front entrance there was a red carpet. On either side of this were hundreds of children with their parents. 'Must be the kids who are going to the new school,' Jason thought. There was a loud murmur through the crowd. The Princess was leaving the building. All eyes in the crowd were looking towards the school doors. No one seemed to notice him. He jumped up so as to see above the heads.

The Princess, closely followed by her detective and lady-in-waiting, was moving

along the red carpet.

Without any hesitation, Jason leapt. His leap took him above the heads of the children and their parents to land upright on the red carpet. He looked up and found himself face to face with the Princess.

'Oh,' she gasped, dropping her bouquet of flowers. Her hand went to her face and she looked a little frightened.

'What's going on here?' said the detective, pushing himself between Jason and the Princess. A size-ten police boot came down accidentally on Jason's unprotected flipper.

'Ow,' cried Jason, not being able to hold back from the pain of it. Tears welled in his eyes and he began to cry. Great sobs issued from Jason. The tears brought on by the pain in his flipper were increased as he re-lived the sadness of the previous few days.

The detective looked embarrassed. 'Sorry,' he said sheepishly. The Princess leaned forward, looking intently at Jason.

'Please don't cry,' she said, touching him lightly on the shoulder. 'Is there something I can do?'

'Please, Princess,' stammered Jason, his tears suddenly gone, 'I need to be kissed by a real princess.'

'Well,' she said, glancing uneasily at her detective.

Jason whispered, 'Please, Princess, I need to be kissed because . . .' and then briefly the whole story came pouring out.

The Princess stood there patiently until he had finished. Then, without a word, she leaned forward and kissed him gently on the forehead. There was a flash of light and standing in place of the frog was Jason the boy. A young man in the crowd gave Jason his large Union Jack to wrap round him, and the Princess, looking slightly pale, said, 'I just can't wait to tell the boys all about this.' With a quick wave to Jason she was whisked away by her detective and lady-in-waiting.

Jason found himself alone at the edge of the crowd. Gratefully he still clung to the Union Jack the young man had given him.

Then he started his journey home, the flag held tightly in place. Suddenly he thought of his parents. 'I wonder if it has

worked for them,' he thought. His heart sank at the thought that they might still be frogs. Seeing a telephone box, he hurried to it. After reversing the charges, he finally heard his mother's voice. 'Are you OK, mum?' he asked.

'Oh yes, Jason, your father and I are back to our normal selves. Are you?'

'Yes, mum,' he cried happily.

'Then hurry home, son,' his mother replied.

Jason rushed from the telephone box. He could not wait to see his parents normal again. His thoughts drifted to his little brother. 'Mum didn't mention him, and I didn't ask if he was normal again. Oh, I do hope he is.'

Then a big grin spread across his face. 'I dunno,' he said out loud. 'It would be fun to watch him grow legs.'

THE END